Dedicated to Olivia Weatherford

Our best friend

Olivia Weatherford,the best person ever.

Contents

↜1↝
The Night Before

"I am so excited for the first day tomorrow!!!!"squealed Maddie.It was the night before their first day of middle school.

"So am I,"replied Maple.

"Will you please be quiet?I am trying to sleep!" Mia asked,with a bit of anger in her voice.Those are the Carson triplets every night before they go to bed.Maddie being energetic,Maple being a nerd,and Mia being a loudmouth and getting angry really easily.All of the them had blond hair,blue eyes,and a lot more in common.They were often confused by their friends and teachers.Thier parents after a while figured out how tell them apart.

"Lights out girls!"shouted Mrs.Carson.

"Okay Mom!"Maple shouted back,with Mia grunting and Maddie laughing in the background.

In the morning the triplets were frantic to get to school.

"OMG!I have know idea what to wear for the first day of middle school!"shouted Maddie.

"Why did you take my blouse!"screamed Maple.

"Will you stop arguing for once!I'm still trying to sleep"Mia angrily screeched.

"You are not the mom here,but yes,everyone get situated and calm down,"said Mrs.Carson patiently,as she pulled the blouse out of Maddie's hands and handed it to Maple.

"Get out of bed lazy bum,"Mrs.Carson said to Mia.

Finally the triplets came out their bedroom door dressed and ready for breakfast.

"Waffles are ready.Girls,come down stairs,"Mrs.Carson told the girls.All of the girls raced down the stairs and greedily chomped down their waffles.Then, they headed to the car so they could drive to a so-called excellent day.

∼2∼
The Worst Day

They all got into the car and buckled up for their first day of middle school.

"I don't know why but I feel really nervous and sick, my stomach is hurting and my head is too,"Maddie whispered softly.Mrs.Carson held her hand tightly.

"It will be okay,"Mrs.Carson said warmly, "We are almost there!"she added to make Maddie feel better.

Soon enough they arrived at Athens Middle School.

"Wow I can't believe how big it is,"Maple said.

"Me too,"Mia remarked, amazed.Maddie was sitting quietly in her seat wondering what the day would be like.

When they pulled up in front of the school, they all tumbled out of the car trying to be the first one in.

"I can't believe this,"Mia whispered.

"Okay,I have to get to my homeroom class.See you at recess,"Maddie shouted over her shoulder.

"Okay!"replied Maple and Mia

As recess approached,the triplets met up and walked to the playground together.They walked to the pavilion. "I am a little dizzy,"Maddie groaned

Then,out of nowhere,she fell to the ground unresponsive of her name.

"Maddie!"Maple and Mia screamed.Their friend Paisley ran over to the teachers and reported the incident.The teachers ran over and called Mr.and Mrs.Carson then,911.An ambulance came almost immediately.

They loaded Maddie into the ambulance and took her to the hospital.After school Maple and Mia went to the hospital to see their sister.Their parents came out and told them that the doctors were running tests on Maddie to see what happened.

"But,for now you have to go home with your dad," Mrs.Carson informed them. "No mom.Please let us stay,we are her sister,"Mia begged.

"No,"Mrs.Carson replied sternly,"Doctors orders,"she added with a laugh.

At home the girls were trying to figure out what had happened to Maddie.

"Do you think she was allergic to something?"Maple said anxiously.

"No, I think she just got dizzy and will be fine,"Mia added,"I hope."The girls were up all night thinking about what happened to their sister.The next morning they would be aloud to visit their sister to see what happened.So they got up early [well at least Maple did] to get ready.Mia and Maple got ready and ate their breakfast then watched part of a movie until it was time to go.

"Come on Dad,it's time to go, we're going to be late!" Maple and Mia screamed at their dad

"Ok,ok I will be there in a sec.Get in the car for now,"Mr.Carson replied.The girls and their dad got into the car

∽3∿
What!?

Soon enough they got to the hospital.They were surprised to see their mom all teared up.Mr.Carson went into Maddie's hospital room so Mrs.Carson could explain to him.The girls overheard a bit of their conversation.

"Should we tell the girls?"Mr.Carson whispered. "Yes,it is their sister you know,"Mrs.Carson whispered back.

The girls were more curious than ever before.Their parents came out and told them… "Your sister has cancer,"Mrs.Carson whispered.

"WHAT!"the two screamed.Then, burst into tears.Mia threw her arms around her mother's waist.

"She will be transferred to St.Jude,"Mrs.Carson added,trying not to look them in the eye.

"But why?"Maple wondered.Before she got an answer,a doctor came telling Mr. and Mrs.Carson that the ambulance had arrived.

Mr.Carson drove Maple and Mia home, both of the girls' faces stained red for the night.The next day they had to go back to school.

"I don't want to go to school without Maddie,"Mia whispered.Thats all either of them said all morning.They just sat there all class, everyone staring at them and trying to ask what happened to Maddie.The girls just wished for everything to go back to normal.

"Can I tell Everly the news?"the triplets best friend Paisley asked."Sure,"Maple replied. Mia was too busy staring at the wall looking at a poster that said,"Keep Your Hopes Up For Maddie".

"How do they know?"Mia whispered to Maple.

"Probably,Mom and Dad,"Maple said with a sigh.After school their dad came to pick them up to see Maddie.

When they got to St.Jude,Maddie was propped up in her bed reading.They took another look at her and realized she was bald.The girls did not know what to say about their sister.Mrs.Carson looked at Mr.Carson and he shrugged.

"Why didn't you tell them?"she whispered sternly.

"I thought they already knew,"Mr.Carson whispered back.The girls said "hi"to Maddie,then just stood there looking at her, shocked.

Then Maddie said,"I know you are shocked that I am bald.It's written all over your faces."

"But I never wrote on my face,"said Mia trying to make Maddie laugh.It worked.Maddie laughed so hard that anyone could hear her.

Eventually they had to go home. It was friday night both their parents were staying with Maddie for the night the girls will be by themselves.

~4~
Just The Two Of Us

Back at their house Mia and Maple were alone and miserable. They missed their mom and dad but most of all they missed Maddie.It was a saturday morning usually saturdays were fun but not this one.Usually they would be chatting with Maddie or listening to her dad jokes.

"Now,Saturday is sooooo boring,"Mia mumbled.

"I know,"Maple began."And all because of something we can't even help."Maple ran over to her phone ready to text their mom but Mrs.Carson had beaten her to it.She texted that Maddie had to get surgery and that they would have to be alone for a couple more days.

Maple shared the news with Mia.Then out of nowhere Mia burst into tears.Maple tried to calm her down,then asked."What is the matter."

"I just wish things could go back to normal,"she cried.

"Me too but you don't see me crying do you,"Maple admitted.Then Mia made a comment that made Maple cry.

"Don't you feel like we're only twins now?"whispered Mia to Maple.Maple could not help herself.She burst into tears like Mia had before.

"Yeah I do,"she whispered back.
In a couple of days they would get to see Maddie.

"What can I wear?"Maple asked.

"Wear your new pink shirt with the cancer ribbon on it and some black pants.I will wear mine too,"Mia shouted,acting like Maple was a baby.

"Ok,know it all,"Maple screamed back.Then Mia ran up to their room and locked the door.

"I'm sorry please come out,"Maple pleaded.Maple kept begging her to come out.When she finally did they went into the kitchen and got some leftover soup and heated it up.When it was done Mia shouted Maple down for dinner.She was upstairs packing their suitcases so they could visit Maddie.

Mia and Maple both thought about Maddie all day and in their dreams at night they even thought about her in school.They would never forget Maddie no matter what happened.

Then Mia said,"Do you think that Maddie might die?"Maple paused then answered, "The world is a place of possibilities but there is still hope even in darkness.I can't tell you for sure but even so,I still have you."Mia got up and threw her arms around Maple.She practically squeezed the guts out of Maple.

"Geez girl your breath reeks, what did you brush your teeth with old sardines and onions!"Maple screamed."No it is called garlic soup for your information,"Mia said back.Maple thought whatever it was stinked no matter what.

Later on their dad came to pick them up to see Maddie.The drive there felt like eternity they were desperate to see Maddie.

They felt like they had not seen Maddie for a year."Why has it been so long,dad?"Maple questioned her father on their car ride."Since what?"he asked.

"Since we've seen Maddie,"Mia piped in.Their dad looked very sad.

"Maddie needs treatment a lot so you can't see her very often,but she doesn't have it today,"he said honestly and with happiness but also sadness.

⌁5⌁
The Grand Tour

They hugged Maddie as hard as they could when they got there.They never realized how much they loved Maddie until she got cancer.Then they pulled out Maddie's favorite stuffed bear that she left at home.She snuggled it hard as she could.

She thanked them and when the doctor came in she said,"Why,looks like I have a guest today,"looking at Maddie's stuffed bear.

"Indeed you do,"Maddie replied with a big smile.
The doctor was very pleased that Maddie was happy.Then she noticed Maple and Mia.

"Welcome,"she said grinning from ear to ear,"Would you like a tour of St.Jude?".Maddie smiled and the doctor nodded towards her. She practically jumped from her hospital bed with excitement.

"First,the nail salon,"Maddie practically Explained in a sassy way,"That is where I have been getting my nails done"."So this is where you've been getting all those adorable watermelon nails!"Maple exclaimed.
They were very excited; they have never been around St.Jude.There parents let them be so they could get work done and so that Maddie could give Maple and Mia a tour.Later that day after they had talked about school and things like that for a while Maddie got up to start the tour.

They went out of her room and to the salon where they got the cutest nails ever.Then they went to the pizza place and the cafe because it was about lunch time.Lets just say it was the best meal they ever had.Then they went to the bowling alley.Maddie won every time.

"I have been practicing," Maddie admitted.The girls giggled.Finally,they went to the school with all the kids who had cancer that were not well enough to go to actual school.Maple and Mia looked sad. Maddie saw them and asked them what was wrong.

The girls said,"It is just sad that they can't go to real school because they are so sick".

Maddie was about to say something when the fire alarm went off. The girls ran outside as fast as they could; they were scared to death.They stood outside with all the other patients.Was St.jude burning down?All the other patients looked sad.How could they get the care they needed without the hospital?Then a few minutes later,someone came out and said it was a false alarm.Everyone sighed with relief.Someone must have accidentally pressed it.All the people returned to what they were doing.Then

Mr.and Mrs.Carson ran to the girls asking if they were okay.

Then they said that they needed to go home and that they would be back to see Maddie soon.

↜6↝
Surprise!!!!

They were getting ready to go see
Maddie and surprise her for their birthday.

"I am so excited to see her
reaction,"said a very excited Maple.

"Same here,"replied Mia very
calmly.They were at the store getting a present
for Maddie.They had looked at
dolls,puzzles,and books.But none of them
seemed right.Mia stuffed something into her
pocket.They looked for a couple more
minutes.All the while,Mia had a strange smile
on her face.Maple wondered what was going
on with her until Mia screamed,"Guys I got it!".

"What do you got?"asked Mrs.Carson
curiously.Mia smiled as she pulled something
out of her pocket.It was amazing. They knew

Maddie would love it. They all grinned from ear to ear.

But, they needed to go drive to St.Jude to surprise Maddie for her birthday party. They headed home to get their bags. They arrived just on time with her present and cake waiting to scream "surprise" to her when she came back from chemo. Soon enough Maddie walked back in the room sad and lonely. They jumped out from wherever they were hiding and screamed "Surprise!".

She screamed and looked over then a smile formed over her face she said,"I thought I would have to spend this birthday alone".Then she looked around again and saw the decorations,cards,presents,and the cake.Another smile formed on her face as she hugged her mom and dad then Maple and Mia.

She saw Maple and Mia's bags then said,"What do you need those for?".

Maple smiled,"We are staying the night".Maddie smiled again for the one hundredth time today.They went to the pizza place to eat and then came back to her room to eat cake and sing happy birthday.She opened her presents and when she saw the card from her family and what it had inside it she screamed.It was tickets to Disney world!Then, she hugged all of them again,and smiled.She got a lot of money and other things because other people sent her gifts as well.Nurses from the hospital stopped by to see what was going on.They cheered seeing one of their favorite patients so happy.

Maddie said it was the best Friday she has had since she came to St.Jude.The girls have not seen her that happy for a while.The thought that she was happy made them happy.They watched a movie[Charlotte's Web,Maddie's favorite].Then went to bed exhausted from the day they had.They woke up in the middle of the night of Maddie screaming,"Wake up,wake up".Maple and Mia jumped out of their sleeping bags."What is happening!"Mia shouted."We're officially thirteen!"Maddie squealed."That's what you woke us for,"Mia groaned as Maple chuckled in the background.

They went back to sleep and woke up the next morning very hungry.Maddie said,"Come on let's go to the cafe for some breakfast".Their parents had rented a hotel room nearby the hospital.They said that they would give the girls some alone time together.Maple,Maddie,and Mia went down to the cafe to get breakfast.Maddie got the biggest stack of pancakes they had ever seen.Mia got some bacon and a bagel.Maple got three hard boiled eggs and some toast.

They knew that their time together would come to an end very soon when their parents got here.They wished it would never end.Last night had been.More fun than they have had for what seemed like forever.

ᔕ 7 ᔐ

A Parent's

Perspective

While the girls were having fun,their parents were in a luxury hotel enjoying themselves.Well,not what you would call "enjoying".You would think they were,but boy your wrong.They spent their entire time worrying about the girls back at St.Jude.They were unable to enjoy themselves at all.

The girls were taking some time off of school because of what happened to Maddie.She has had cancer for three months.To her parents it felt like eternity.

"Do you think the girls are alright?"asked Mrs.Carson for the fifth time that day.

"Yes I am sure they are,"Mr.Carson reassured her,"You need to stop worrying about them."

"Sorry it's just I don't know what they're doing and I want to be there too,"Mrs.Carson stuttered in one breath.

"It's ok.Now let's get some breakfast in the parlor,"Mr.Carson told her.

They went on the elevator and into the parlor.Mrs.Carson gripped Mr.Carson's hand,digging her fingernails into his skin.

"Wow,you don't have to hold my hand that hard!"Mr.Carson explained.Mrs.Carson put an apologetic look on her face.

"It's okay,"Mr.Carson laughed.

They arrived at the breakfast bar.You could have eggs,bacon,grits,toast,waffles,pancakes, cereal,and pretty much anything breakfasty you could think of.The two gasped at all the choices.

In the end, Mrs. Carson had eggs, bacon, and toast. Mr. Carson had two waffles, grits, and bacon. They were very full.

Then, after waiting a bit, they put their swimsuits on. The indoor pool just opened after construction, so they went for a swim. Mr. Carson cannon balled into the pool, soaking Mrs. Carson. She laughed with terror.

"Sorry, honey," Mr. Carson shouted.

"All good," Mrs. Carson began. But, before she could finish, a shout rang from the other side of the pool. Every one turned their heads in the direction of the shout. What they saw took their breath away. A young girl, maybe around five years old, was falling into the water. It did not look like a game, if it was. Without hesitation, Mr. Carson dove underneath the surface, returning on the other side of the pool, the little girl in his arms. Her mother screeched with delight of the sight of seeing her daughter again.

"Lily!"She cheered.She ran to lily and Mr.Carson and grabbed lily out of his arms.When Mr.Carson swam back to Mrs.Carson,she congratulated him.

"Nicely done,"she weakly smiled,impressed.

"Thanks,"Mr.Carson said,disappointed that his own girls were not there.

Mrs.Carson sighed heavily. "I want to know that my own girls are okay,"she grunted,shaking her head disapprovingly.She wanted to pick up her phone and call Maddie's nurse,to make sure they were all right but,she decided to just relax and that it would only cause trouble to the triplets fun sleepover.

Before Mr.Carson could respond,Lily's mom
ran over.

"Sir-sir,"she stuttered,"Are you the one who saved my daughter?".

"Yes,"Mr.Carson replied.

"Do you know where the nearest doctor is?"she asked.

"No sorry.I am not familiar with the area,"Mr.Carson said.

Then she went off to help her daughter,who was still recovering from what had happened.Mrs.Carson checked her watch and looked startled.Then she nearly screamed,"We are going to be late to pick up the girls.They both ran inside the hotel got dressed then headed straight to the car with all of their luggage.When they got to St.Jude Mrs. and Mr.Carson went on the elevator to the lobby.

Of course Mia and Maple begged to stay longer but were still happy to see their parents.

"We don't want to go home,"Mia screamed angrily.

"Yeah,"Maple exclaimed, "Let us stay".

The girls kept begging and begging but their parents were firm about it."Absolutely not.You guys are acting like two year olds.Be more mature.Besides,you will.be back to see Maddie very soon,"Mrs.Carson scolded.

"Bye!Tell Paisley and Everly I miss them!"Maddie called after them.

⌢8⌢
Pink Day!

Back at school,they had a pink day in honor of Maddie.The principal asked that everyone wore the shirt that had the cancer ribbon or something pink.

"Excuse me students,"the principal called over the intercom.

Mrs.jackson shushed Mia and Maple's home room class.The two sisters knew what the principal was about to say.They looked up from their morning work and glued their ears to the cracking intercom.

"We thank those who wore pink in honor of our very own Maddie Carson!At this time,can we get her sisters,Maple and Mia,to the office?And don't forget to tell your parents about the parade we're holding for Maddie.It will be here at 6:00.There will be shirts,food,and plenty more fun!And,we will see

Maddie for the first time in a long time!"the principal boomed.

Maple and Mia rose to go but their teacher stopped them in their tracks.

"Everybody please give a round of applause to Maple and Mia because,"she paused,"because it can be hard having a sister with cancer.But,they're doing a great job."

With that everyone stood up and clapped until their hands turned red.The two smiled and thanked their wonderful teacher.They got lots of high fives and cheerful comments but,the end was the best.

Mrs.Jackson knelt down on one knee and looked them straight in the eye.

"I really meant what I said,"she began,"to be honest,my sister had cancer,too.It was hard.Some times I had an emotional breakdown.I've never seen you girls do that.I am amazed.You girls rock."Both girls left the room with tears in their eyes.

In the office,both girls were welcomed by a goody bag filled with candy and small cute toys.They thanked the secretary,who directed them to the principal's office.When they arrived,Maple nearly screeched.Mia gasped.The room was full of pink streamers and balloons.Pictures of the triplets sat in frames on the floor.

"What is all this for?"Mia asked the principal,who was slouched at her desk covered in papers and folders.

"Your mom dropped it off for tonight.Thats why you're here,to help me and the members of P.T.O. decorate this school.Don't worry,we have plenty more stuff than just this.And when I say "stuff",I mean "stuff","she explained.They all giggled.And,by the end of second period,the place looked awesome.

ᔓ9ᔓ
The Parade

Back at home the girls could barely wait.They thought they were going to die.They were both so excited and impatient.Just then,they heard a knock on the door.It was their mom.And,she had just done some last minute shopping for the parade.She had bought things like candy and more decorations for the school.

"This is going to be a great night.The school is going to see your sister for the first time in a while,"Mrs.Carson almost screamed because she was so excited.

"I know!I am so excited!"Mia screamed.

"Me too!"Maple screamed.

So the girls and their mom drove to the school to help set up the parade.Soon enough the first guests started arriving.

"The party has officially started!"Mia bellowed,mocking the intercom voice.

Eventually there were about a hundred people there and there was still more to come.

"Maddie should be here soon,right Mom?"Maple wondered.

"Yeah,she should,"Mrs.Carson replied.

Minutes had passed but there was still no sign of Maddie.Then Mrs.Carson got a text from Mr.Carson,who was with Maddie.Mrs.Carson gasped.The girls looked at her with worry in their eyes.Mrs.Carson looked up at them.Immediately they knew that was something was wrong.

Then Mia said, "She is not coming, is she?"

"I am afraid not,"Mrs.Carson said back with a bit of sorrow in her voice.

"What happened?"Maple asked

"Maddie randomly got sick, so the nurses want her to stay at St.Jude,"Mrs.Carson said honestly.

"Will she ever be normal again?!"Maple screamed angrily.

Then she ran off to what they think is the girls bathroom.They found her nearly an hour later.She was crying and her face was so red that it looked like she was crying the entire hour.Mrs.Carson sat down beside her to comfort her.Then she got a feeling that they all wanted her to be better and normal.

Then Mrs.Carson said, "You have got to know that nobody is normal.Every one is weird or different in a way."

"You're right I never thought of that.But I guess I just want Maddie to be healthy and happy,"Maple just barely managed to slip out.

"She is happy,"Mrs.Carson said back to Maple.

Then out of nowhere Mia [who was currently forgotten] said, "No she is not."

"You may not know it but we do,"Mia said. "She might have not told us talking wise but mentally she did."

"You are right.I felt the same way,"Maple said honestly.

Then,Mrs.Carson said,"You know what? Sometimes she can be sad.I get that.But,everyone is sad sometimes.You have to learn that there's always going to be sadness and you just have to push through and get over it so that you can be happy."

Just then their friend Paisley found them and said,"There you are.Everyone has been looking all over for you.Come on.The parade is so much fun. Let's go play."

So that is what they did when they entered the room that everyone was in.All of the people cheered for them.Maple and Maddie started smiling.They were really happy.They went over to the place where they were giving out pizza and got themselves some.After that they went over to the cake and filled their plates.It was delicious.

This was the best parade they had ever been to.But,when their mom said it was time to leave shortly after they got food the girls were stunned.

"The party is over.We spent a lot longer by the bathroom than you think,"Mrs.Carson admitted.

So they went home to pack to go to see Maddie.Both the girls were scared.They were scared for their sister.

↜10↝
Saved by a Tear

The girls arrived at St.Jude late at night.They headed towards Maddie's room to surprise her.They were excited but nervous at the same time.Apparently,this was the worst she had been since she got cancer,which was six months ago.To Maple and Mia it felt like eternity.They walked in the room.To the girls surprise Maddie was hooked up to oxygen tubes and other stuff.Mia and Maple began to cry.They kept crying until their mom said,"girls,Maddie is fine.She is having trouble breathing and is in pain.Other than that she is fine.She's going to live."

At that moment,Maddie let out a groan.A nurse who was walking down the hall stopped by to see if she was alright.The nurse adjusted some of the equipment.Maddie was better after that but she did not look fine.Around her eyes were purple.The hair that she had grown back was now gone.Maybe she did feel okay but she looked like she was doing horrible.This upset Maple and Mia even more.Then,the nurse went to speak with Mrs.Carson.

"We did some x-rays and we found something unwanted.She does still have cancer yes,but she was born with that."she began.

"Yes,I knew that.You told when she got diagnosed,"Mrs.Carson interrupted.

"Ww-e-ell,we discovered that her cancer is getting worse.If it continues there is a possible chance of death.," the nurse finished.Mrs.Carson gasped.The girls,who were eavesdropping,burst into tears,along with their mother.The thought of their sister dying was devastating.They had been together since they were born,and their mom was very depressed,too.It was 12:00 at night but they were all awake.

Eventually,Mrs.Carson led the girls to bed.She fell asleep not long after.Mr.Carson had been getting Dunkin the entire time.He returned with two dozen donuts,three boxes of munchkins[twenty per container],and two iced coffees.He could barely hold it all!But,the girls had a good breakfast,despite the fact that their mom said it was way to much sugar and that they shouldn't eat a lot.

"I dont care"Maddie whispered to Maple and Mia,interfering with what Mrs.Carson had told them.Maple and Mia copied her.Mrs.Carson was not too happy,but she let them do it anyway.

The only problem was that Maddie was getting to a point where she looked like she was going to die.She was growing weaker and didn't do as much.When Maple and Mia offered to play the game of Life with her,she refused.This caused the girls to be upset.Mrs.Carson reassured them saying that Maddie was just growing sicker and more tired.There wasn't much they could do besides letting her rest.Mrs.Carson did not realize how hard that was for Maple and Mia.

"Girls,leave Maddie alone.She needs some rest!"Mrs.Carson laughed.

"No,Mom.I want to play,"Maddie interupted.She argued that she did not need rest,but Mrs.Carson won,joined by some of Maddie's nurses.So she rested [for three hours!].When she woke up,she was whining.The nurses told Maple and Mia that they needed to step outside the room for a moment.Although they were upset,they obeyed.

"I wonder what is happening in there?"Mia wondered,her ear pressed against the door.

"I think something is happening to Maddie,"Maple guessed.

"WHAT IF SHE IS GOING TO DIE!!!!"Mia screamed,a little bit too loud.The adults inside heard her.Mrs.Carson came out of Maddie's room and tried to calm Mia down some.

She said, "Calm down.People from outside the building could hear you.And Maddie can too.You are scaring her."

Mrs.Carson and the girls went back into Maddie's room and to their surprise,her heart monitor was beeping.The girls hopped on her bed beside her.Maddie's heart monitor let out a long beep.The line that was supposed to be in a zigzag was going in a straight line.Maddie let out her last breath.Maple and Mia wept over her.One of the girls tears landed on her arm.Then something surprising happened.The heart monitor came back on again going in regular zigzags.Everyone was shocked speechless.Maddie let out a gasp and then started breathing normal again.It was a miracle.Everyone let out tears of joy instead of sadness and sorrow.

∿11∿
Better Again!!

Staying alive was not the only big thing that happened.After the tear,we was discovered that Maddie was getting better.Scientists were trying to figure out what happened and why it was possible, but nobody had a clue.Maddie was getting better every day and was almost to the point where she could go home and live a cancer free life!Everyone, even Maddie,was overjoyed when they heard the news.But one thing she would miss,was her new best friend,Riley.Riley was not well enough yet to go home,but Maddie promised to come and visit her often.

"This is like a fairy tale!"Maple said,who was obsessed with princess movies.

"Aren't you a little old to still love princess movies?"Maddie added.

"Sorry Maple but this time I have to agree with Maddie,"Mia remarked.

"It is perfectly fine for girls your age to still like princess movies.As a matter of a fact I still like them myself,

"Okay fine.She can like the stupid princess movies,"Mia groaned.

"They are not stupid.The only thing stupid right now is you!!"Maple shouted back.

"That's because princess movies are not here,"Mia replied without a bit of doubt in her voice.

"Girls!Stop that right now!You do not speak to each other like that."Mrs.Carson shouted above the girls' voices.Maple and Mia stopped,looking at each other with apologetic looks in their eyes.

"That's better,"Mrs.Carson said angrily.The girls were sorry they had made their mom mad.But,Mrs.Carson forgave them.They were all in one piece.

Mr.Carson had no idea what had happened.He got back from work to find a quiet family.Nobody made a peep.Mr.Carson was curious.Most of the time,Mia was shouting and Maple and Maddie were giggling.

To break the silence,Maddie said, "How was your day,Dad?"

"It was fine,thank you,"Mr.Carson replied with a hint of curiosity in his voice.

Then he asked, "What happened?I know something is not right.All of you are too quiet for you to be alright."Nobody answered.

"Ww-ee-ell,Maple and Mia got into a fight," Maddie said honestly. "They were arguing and carrying on about princess movies.Nothing else."

"Okay.Is everybody mad at each other then?"Mr.Carson asked

"No.Just them two but they're calming down,"Maddie explained.Mrs.Carson elaborated saying that she had gotten mad at

them and that was why Maple and Mia were mad at her.Maddie
was the only person not in the fight.

"What do you want me to do about this?"Mr.Carson asked.

"One thing you could do is butt out of this.It is none of your business,"Mia shouted to her father.

Mrs.Carson shouted back at her, "You do not speak to your father like that!Now go into the other room and think about what you just said and when you can control yourself,come out and apologize to your dad."

Maple and Maddie were silent.They were nervous just like every kid was when their parents were cross.Mia let out a sob of frustration;got up and stormed to the other room.She stayed in there for a couple hours,with her parents and sisters left grumpy in the other room.

↜12↝
Back To School

Eventually,after the nurses ran more tests on her,Maddie was able to return home to Athens so she could go back to school.She was overjoyed to hear that said.So were her sisters.

"I can't believe this is actually happening!"Mia screeched.

"Me either!"Maple and Maddie chorused.

"Girls,calm down,"Mrs.Carson whined for the hundredth time.The girls were getting ready for bed on a Sunday night.Once Mrs.Carson had left,they burst into whispers.

"This feels like the day before middle school.Except,something terrible is not going to happen tomorrow,"Maddie said almost nervously.

"Well,you never know what might happen.But hopefully nothing goes wrong tomorrow,"Mia said, with a bit of nervousness in her voice as well.

Then Maple,sounding a bit cross,said,"Nothing is going to happen tomorrow, it will be absolutely perfect."

"Well,as I said,you never know what might happen,"Mia said.

"GO TO SLEEP!"Mrs.Carson yelled,storming into the room.The girls looked up at their outraged mom.They quickly lied down on their bed and closed their eyes.

"Better,"Mrs.Carson mumbled tiredly.After that,the girls sort of slept the entire night.In the morning,they were strangely grumpy.Mrs.Carson recognized and said, "Your grumpy because you went to bed too late and did not get enough sleep."

The girls knew their mom was right but did not want to admit it.They ate breakfast which was waffles just like on the first day of school.Then when they were all ready, they hopped in the car to go to back to school.Maddie has not been to school for just over six months.Maple and Mia had not been at their school since the parade.The girls stepped out of the car and went inside their school.To their surprise,they saw a huge sign that said "WELCOME BACK,MADDIE!!!"Maddie was so happy,she almost screamed.Every body showed Maddie great hospitality.Though Maple and Mia were excited, Maddie was the most excited about being back.

When the day was over she was sad,but excited.She knew she would have to wait a little longer before going back to school again.The reason why she was excited for school ending was because the next day she was going to Disneyland and school ending for the day was just a sign of the trip nearing.

"Hey girls,"Mrs.Carson greeted."How was your day?"

"Awesome!!!!!!!!"Maddie cried.Maple and Mia nodded their heads in agreement.Maddie continued to tell their mother every little detail about her [and Maple and Mia's]day

"Alright.Let's pack some bags,"Mrs.Carson said,rolling up her sleeves with a determined look on her face.

↜13↝
Road Trip!

The girls came down stairs for breakfast so excited they could hardly eat.It was going to be an amazing trip they were almost sure of.When the girls saw that nothing was on the counter they were surprised.

"Where's breakfast?"Maddie asked in a disgusted voice.

"Yeah"Maple and Mia complained to Maddie.

"Breakfast is not here.We are going to eat at Chick-Fil-A "Mrs.Carson yelled,jumping out of the living room. The girls jumped because their mom had scared them big time.Maple and Maddie screamed.Mia just giggled.

After they ate breakfast they got into the car with all their bags and snacks so that they could get going on their drive to disneyland.The girls could hardly wait this trip was going to be the best one yet.Eventually they had stopped and picked up their breakfast which was Chick-Fil-A.The girls each got an eight count of chicken minis,their dad got a huge breakfast burrito,and finally,their mom got a chicken biscuit.They ate everything they got and everyone agreed that it was delicious.

Eventually the girls and their mom fell asleep while Mr.Carson was driving.He wanted to sleep,but he couldn't.When Maddie woke up she checked with her dad to see how much time was left till they got to their hotel.

"There are five minutes left till we get there,"Mr.Carson replied.When Maddie heard that she woke up her sisters and her mom and told them that there was only five minutes until they got to their hotel.Maple,Maddie,and Mia all squealed of joy their mom groaned she did not want to be woke up.

"We are going to Disneyland!We are going to Disneyland.In your face people who

are not going to Disneyland!!,"Mia screamed
out of the car window.

Then Mrs.Carson said,sounding a bit annoyed,
"That is quite enough Maple,and it was also
very mean."

"Hey I'm not Maple!"Mia pouted.

"I'm so tired I don't even know my own
kids names!"Mrs.Carson laughed,trying to
make it clear that she was just talking to
Mr.Carson.

"That's when you know for a fact that
you are tired,"Mia grumbled.

"We all are tired.Lets go and check into
our hotel to get some rest,"Mr.Carson
grumbled,trying to lessen the arguing.Mia was
getting extra mad because she was really tired
like everyone else.It was not helping anyone
full any better [but mainly her tired
parents].They worked constantly trying to calm
her down.

And none of it worked.All of the girls had
started seeing a counsler.Maddie and Maple

had started calming down a bit.Mia seemed to be getting worse.Going to Disney,however,had somewhat cheered her up.She had just started to feel very strong emotions.Mia also had seemed a bit disturbed by this fact.Sleeping had become her new favorite hobby.

"SLEEP!"Mia yelled excitedly.Maddie and Maple glanced at each other nervously.The triplets used to hate going to bed!It was strange for her to change her likes and dislikes so quickly.

"You used to be the child that always slept in and slept the entire night,Mia.And,you've had plenty of other changes.Are you sure that you're alright?"Mrs.Carson asked as they pulled into the parking lot at the hotel.

"I am fine,for pete's sake!"Mia yelled.She pressed the button to open the door and then charged out of the car.Mr.Carson,who was sitting in front of the car,ran after her.She ran to a nearby tree and squatted down beside it.Mr.Carson walked over calmly and stood above her.

"What's up,Mia?"he asked.Mia just sat there,nearly in tears.

Back in the car,the girls were torn up seeing their sister raging like she did.

"Let's just go check into the hotel,"Mrs.Carson suggested.The girls dragged themselves out of the car.They looked helplessly at Mia and Mr.Carson.

Once in the hotel room,the girls were excited again.The hotel mainly consisted of two sets of bunk beds,a king size bed,a kitchen,and a small living room.It also contained an amazing view of...Disney World!!Maple and Maddie oohed and aahed over the window.Mrs.Carson peered over their heads and gasped at the sight.At that moment,Mia barged through the door in tears with Mr.Carson at her heels.She came over to tell Maple and Maddie that she needed to talk to them.Once Mia saw the view she was sort of happy again and Mr.Carson was amazed.

It was getting pretty late.So they went down to the lobby to eat dinner then after that they would go straight to bed because they needed energy to go to Disney World the next day.

It was the next day and all the girls were awake and dressed.Their parents were still sleeping but they were about to wake them up.Each one of them had made themselves breakfast.They were ready to go but there was just one problem.Their parents were still asleep.They could not get to Disney World without their parents to drive them and guard them.So Maple,Maddie,and Mia all tiptoed into their parents room and then they yanked open the curtains.

"Rise and shine,"Mia screamed.Mr.Carson and Mrs.Carson practically jumped through the roof;they were definitely not expecting that to happen.

"I'm up,I'm up!"Mr.Carson said with a yawn.Then he turned over to make Mrs.Carson get her out of bed.Very soon after they were ready to go.It was going to be a good day and they all knew it.

↜14↝
Disney World

In about five minutes.they were in the car on their way to Disney World.The entire drive there the girls talked about how excited they were.Soon enough,they were there.Nobody could believe the sight.They were standing in front of a famous amusement park,watching the roller coaster cars roll by with people screeching inside.The sight of a little girl with pigtails win a prize at one of the games.It had been a while since Maddie had seen a sight like it,because she had been stuck up in a hospital room.

She pulled her ponytail out of her hair and let the breeze blow the thick blond hair away.She felt like she had just been freed from prison.The hospital room had been cheerful,but not a place she wanted to be at.

"Let's go to the spot with princesses first,"Maple suggested.Mia and Maddie agreed.They found a pamphlet and pointed out where they would be going.On the walk there,they stopped for ice cream and lemonade.Mr.Carson had booked warm days for their trip.The girls had sweat dripping down their faces.In fact,practically everyone the Carson family walked by was full of sweat and had red faces.But they were too excited to care.

Once they were at the Royal Hall which is where the princesses are, all of the girls ran to their favorite princess.

It was not very busy since it was a Tuesday.They had the entire place to themselves besides another family with a small girl and a baby boy.The workers said that this is the least busy it has been for decades[on the days that it was open].They also said that Tuesday was never super busy,since it was in the middle of the week and all the kids were usually in school.Maple,Maddie,and Mia had missed so much school that year that the teachers didn't even care anymore.But the bad part about that is if they don't pass the final exams they have to repeat sixth grade. But,they did not worry about it.They were sure that they would pass.They were pretty smart kids and the extra knowledge was sure to help them.

Maddie ran to Belle,her favorite princess.Maple ran to Arial.Mia ran over to Rapunzel,tripping along the way.The only reason Mia liked Rapunzel is because she hits people with a frying pan.After they talked to the princesses for a bit they headed over to Animal Kingdom.There was so much to do they could not decide in the end they all went somewhere different.Since the park was basically empty their parents let them wonder off by themselves as long as they stayed in Animal Kingdom.After they had spent at least four hours in Animal Kingdom their parents said it was time for them to go back to the hotel because it was getting late. They got their stuff and headed to the car. But they still had tomorrow to come back and enjoy themselves.

↶15↷
{Epilogue}

One year later

It had been a whole 12 months since Maddie was released from the hospital and was titled cancer free.They were living a "normal life" but really no one's life is normal.

One day Maddie went out to check the mail.She found an interesting letter that was different from all the others.

She ran in and told her mom, "I think that the group of scientists who were trying to find out what saved me sent us a letter."

"Let me open it in case it's something private or something you girls don't need to know about,"Mrs.Carson said.Maddie handed the letter to her.Mrs.Carson opened it up and read through it carefully she had a surprised look on her face then her expression went back to normal.

She read aloud the letter.It said,

"Dear Mr and Mrs.Carson,We sort of know how Maddie got better.There is a specific chemical in a tear that removes stress.We are not sure how,but that could have been the reason.I must say,this is one of the craziest things that has happened in history.People all over the world are hearing about this and we have been having to do a lot of interviews with other scientists.Thanks to you guys,we are earning a lot more money and are growing in our careers.As a gift,we are inviting you and your family to come hang out at our lab for a couple days.Specific directions will be mailed soon.

Yours truly,

The scientists at Athens"

"Oh my gosh,"Mrs.Carson gasped and quickly tucked the letter into her pocket.She explained everything to the triplets and they were excited,too.Mr.Carson was happy to see that they had figured out the reason for Maddie's healing and that they would get to go to the laboratory.

"All right!"Mr.Carson shouted,fist-bumbing Maple and Mia and hugging Maddie.The triplets were ecstatic;they couldn't believe that they were going to an actual laboratory sometime soon.

Authors note

You may be wondering why we wrote this book.Here is the complete story.

About a year ago,our best friend passed away from cancer.We grieved deeply. Her family, which contained five people [including Olivia],is kind. Eli,Olivia's brother,is funny and cute.Ella,Olivia's sister,is shy but cute and fun to be around.Sarah,Olivia's mom, is so kind and sweet. Aaron,Olivia's dad, is funny and caring.Olivia was sweet,funny,kind,and the best,best friend.Together they made a perfect family.

There is that part of the story,but you may ask when we decided to put the book into action.Well that takes us back to a field trip in fourth grade.We were going to the Tellus museum and of course,we were sitting next to each other.

Millie explained to Emory that she decided to draft out a small book for her to have.Then,Emory decided to have a book of our own.They made a plan using some yellow sticky notes and a purple pen that Millie had in her fanny pack.

This plan turned into using our recess every day to type this book on the computer.Time was limited since Emory was moving to Alabama and would not be at Candy's Creek in fifth grade.Our close friends read a couple chapters and gave us feedback.With their help,and Mrs.Hubbard [our fourth grade teacher] we made a successful book.Somehow,a lot of people heard about what we were doing.They encouraged us and were determined to learn more.A big thank you to them.And especially to Mrs.Hubbard,who answered all our grammar questions and agreed to us doing this.Without her,you would not be reading this.

And always remember to live like Liv [cause that's a great way to live].

Sincerely

Millie Pusch & Emory Hennessey

Best wishes always

And a special thanks to...

Chase Ann Harvey

Anne Marie Eldridge

Mrs.Hubbard

Nora Branson

Zaby Wilcox

Hatcher Gravelle

And everyone who reads this,we believe in you

Made in the USA
Columbia, SC
28 August 2024

41237799R00039